Set

In

Stone

Memoirs of the Lincoln Imp

By Charles Ullestad

A BIG THANKS to Makena Vargo for the cover's illustration. One of the most brilliant and talented students I've ever had the honor to teach.

This book is
dedicated to
Finn, my son and
little demon
child whom I love
so much.

Greetings from the Author:

Hello,

If you're into history, I do believe you'll thoroughly enjoy this story. If you like to read fiction from the point of view of an unloveable creature such as an imp (demon), then I also think you'll enjoy this story.

This is the story of a stone imp who sits on one of the most impressive cathedrals in history. Not to mention he has a story of how he got there and has his own football (soccer) club named after him. When details of the Imp's life were emailed to me, I was more than intrigued, I was genuinely excited and committed. I immediately put the emails together and wrote his story.

If you would like to reach out to the Imp, don't. He doesn't want you to. That's what his last email to me said anyway.

So enjoy and thank you for reading!

Sincerely,

Charles

Set In: Lincoln, England

Prelude: Some time in the late 12th century

The wind howled that night something fierce. Lightning and thunder followed like they were on the hunt. Everyone in the city of Lincoln was inside their homes this cold, blustery night. They were doing their best to enjoy the warmth and comfort of their beds, or savouring a cup of warm stew by the fire.

There were hardly any souls outside during this storm, with the exception of a stray dog looking for shelter, or some rats looking for food. But there were also two imps out and about this night, running along the roofs of homes and making a mess everywhere they went. Imps are mischievous little demons that try to play pranks and cause trouble wherever they go. Imagine two little devils with tiny little horns on their heads and one can picture an imp.

Who knew what terrors they would try to cause this night.

The imps saw the cathedral in the center of the city, looked to one another, and giggled with delight. They were both thinking the same thing. Causing mayhem in a church would surely give these two creatures nothing but pure happiness, and it would allow them to share several good stories when they returned home. Oh how the Devil and his other minions would laugh and cackle with pleasure at their troublesome tale.

As they neared the cathedral, a strong wind took hold of the two and swept them inside through the great doors. They had planned on going in another way, but this would do. Immediately, they got to work. They began by smashing the stained glass windows along the walls. All of that beautiful artwork now shattered. They went about and blew out all the candles, and broke them in half of course. When the Dean came out of his chambers to see what was happening, one of the imps went and tripped him, making him fall over and hit his head on a pew. He was out cold for the night. The imps were howling with laughter at the scene. One of them even mimicked the dean falling over and making sounds to mock the poor man.

With all of this laughter and the sounds of destroying the inside of the church, an angel awoke and came out of a Bible that had been sitting on top of the altar. When the angel saw what was happening, he ordered the imps to stop. "Wicked imps, be turned to stone!" The imps jumped away from where they had been mocking the unconscious Dean, one of them going under a nearby pew, and the other landing at the top of a stone pillar. The imps were still silent for a moment, having not expected an appearance from the enemy this night.

The imp under the pew hissed to his partner, "let us away back home. We have done enough here."

However, the other imp did not hear his friend or simply

refused to back down. He began mocking the angel, insulting him, and even threw some stones in his direction. The angel, in return, pointed his finger at the imp atop the stone pillar, and could be heard whispering something. Suddenly, as the imp sat laughing with his right leg crossed over his left knee, he turned to stone.

The imp beneath the pew gasped, and in his shock ran out and into the night, never to be seen at the cathedral again. The angel nodded, seemed satisfied, and returned to the Bible for some sleep. The mischievous imp on top of the stone pillar sat there, frozen in stone, and that was that.

Chapter 1: Introducing Myself

You know, being an imp, or a demon as I should probably say to sound more "politically correct," wasn't so bad. I got to run around with my friends, terrorize people, and cause mischief. It was a great life! But who has to come and ruin all of that? That damn angel. Nathaniel. I like to call him Nathan for short, or Nate, but he does not seem to like it, which makes it all the better. Anyway, that stupid angel had to come out that night and ruin it all. Turning me to stone just because I yelled some things at him and threw a stone?

Okay, so it was more than one stone. And I'm quite sure I should not repeat the things I said that night. It would teach the little ones some very naughty words.

My life since that night has been an odd one. I've been stuck here in this cathedral since, what, 1192? 1193? I'm not sure. It was so long ago. And now it's the year 2020. Since then there have been perhaps a few stories or events, but - oh crap! I forgot to introduce myself. How rude.

I have a name that was given to me by the Devil, but I haven't heard it in hundreds of years, so I've sort of forgotten it, but that's okay because it's in demon tongue and you probably wouldn't understand it. Over the last few hundred years I've heard people refer to me as several different things. I've heard "Imp", "Demon", "Grotesque" (I like that one), "Gargoyle", and "Lincoln". I'll pretty much accept any of those names. Nathan, whenever he comes out and about, typically calls me Imp. I think he says it in a derogatory manner, but that's fine with me. For the sake of keeping it simple, I am writing here that my name is Linc. I like the name Linc, and if you don't shut it because I don't care.

Hmm, I should probably write down where I come from and how I'm even able to write this down. Well, to keep it short and sweet, my father was an imp and my mother was a succubus. I don't know how that works so please don't ask. All I know is they got together, yada yada yada, and there I was. I don't remember my mother, but apparently I am what some would consider a larger size of my species because of her. So I'm just about a foot tall, which is fairly large for a sprite, or imp. You have to know that the definition of an imp is a small demon, or sprite. I hate the word sprite though, so I won't refer to myself in that way. I sound like a freaking fairy when I say it. I'm not some cute little fairy that's going to sing and dance with you around the forest.

Now, you might be wondering how I'm moving about and telling my story on paper. Well, a few years after Nathan first turned me to stone, he must have felt remorse and wanted me to apologize or something. I don't know, those angels are all about forgiveness. So he allowed me to actually move and talk. So I'm still stone and my face is stuck in this odd looking smile. Considering the alternative, I suppose I had to accept it. There was a catch with this, however. Nathan told me that I was never allowed to leave the cathedral grounds, and I could not interfere or interact with any of the humans. Ugh, boring, but fine.

So anyway, I'm writing down my memoirs and telling you the things that I have seen this past millennium. I found an old typewriter back from the Second World War and some paper to go with it in an old unused office, so I don't think anyone will notice it's even missing.

There's something odd going on around the cathedral lately and I need to put it down on paper just in case I'm destroyed, or I break the rules. Let's be honest I am made out of stone now. I can easily shatter or something. My time in Lincoln (that's in England by the way did I say that before? I meant to.) has been interesting.

Chapter 2: Present Day

_____Christmas time. I'm supposed to hate it, you know. But over the last several hundred years I've come to enjoy the festivities that come with this Christian holiday. The songs, the food, the drinking, and the movies! I can't get enough of Home Alone, Arthur Christmas, and of course...The Grinch. I can relate to the guy. I mean gifts and gifts and more gifts. That's what people expect on Christmas Day. Give me a fine roast beef and a glass of Cab Sauvignon while listening to some Nat King Cole on the record player makes me one happy imp. Plus, it's the one day of the year my buddy Nate is in a decent mood.

This Christmas season, I began my Yuletide festivities by watching Polar Express on my iphone with a cup of cocoa. There I was looking out over the snow covered yard in the cloister with a good movie and a warm beverage. It's a wonderful thing to watch the snow fall and grace us with her presence. She dances through the air as if she were a ballerina, and then so gracefully takes a bow and settles on the ground, watching as her human and creature admirers gaze at her in wonder and awe.

As I was just getting to a good part in the movie, I noticed a child running towards the cathedral. I assumed it was a girl because I saw long brown hair escaping parts of the winter cap on her head. It could've been a boy. I just find that statistically that someone with long hair tends to be a girl. I was right, as I sensed something wrong with the child as she came closer and closer. She had pulled her hat off her head by the time she entered the church and was still crying just a bit as she wandered around. Her cheeks were a full red, from both crying and the cold. She had light brown hair, with pale skin and a few freckles scattered here and there. I guessed she was about eight years old or so. She went to a corner of the church and sat down against the wall, as if hoping to be swallowed up into the cathedral. She looked around, and seeing no one around her, pulled up her sleeve on her left arm. There I saw one of the biggest bruises I'd ever seen. She touched it gingerly, cried out at the pain, and slowly pulled the sleeve back down.

I felt her pain and sorrow. I could sense that this was something she had experienced before but was still struggling with it. A bully at school? No it was more personal. She felt guilty for this happening to her, but why?

After crying for a while longer, she left the cathedral with just a few tears dropping down into the snow as she went. The tears became a part of the frozen ballerina and that was that.

Chapter 3: 1215

Before I get to the strange things happening, I want to tell you, random human reader, what my life has been like since Nathan ruined it.

If you're not aware, 1215 is a big year in terms of history. I bet you don't know what I'm referring to, do you? Sounds right, people never seem to learn from history, so they certainly aren't going to remember it. Well, that was the year of the Magna Carta. I'm not about to give a big history lesson here, so relax a second and keep on reading. I'll keep it short. In 1215, King John of England was made to sign the famous document, to bring peace, but more importantly, protect the people of England and hold the King accountable to the law. There, the lesson is done.

But, did you know that a copy of the Carta was brought to Lincoln Cathedral? And, did you know that the king tried to have it destroyed? Think about it, if there's no physical copy of the document, the king cannot be held accountable and he can go about, doing whatever he wants to do.

It turns out King John ordered a knight to go to the cathedral and find out the exact location of the Carta, and if able, destroy it. Otherwise, he was to return and reveal its location to the king. How do I know this? I'm a demon. I can tell

when people have bad intentions,
and then I can basically read
their minds. Plus I have great
eyesight and hearing.

Anywho, this knight walks in,
and right away I can sense it. The
guy is trouble and wants the
Carta. So first, he comes in, hood
over his head and trying not to
draw attention. He decides to
avoid the Bishop, Hugh of Wells
was his name, and goes over to one
of the altar boys. I can hear
their conversation.

Knight: Excuse me boy. This is a
beautiful church. May I ask how
old it is?
Boy: I'm not sure sir. It's been
around since before I was born.
Knight: That's true I suppose. Can
thou tell me where they keep all
of the old books and records?
Boy: I'm not too sure about that
either, but I think I've seen a
lot of books in the Bishop's
quarters.
Knight: And what about the Magna
Carta?

Boy: Well, um… I'm not sure but the Bishop has said to not touch his chests in his office.
Knight: And where is that?
Boy: Behind the altar to the right there.
Knight: Thank you boy. I appreciate your honesty. Keep this conversation to yourself.

And with that, the knight tossed a coin to the boy and walked towards the altar. I watched from my perch as he seemed intent on walking straight into the Bishop's office, but he noticed several men in the cathedral and did not wish to be noticed. There were holy men, nobles, and a few peasants or servants. I could sense that the knight was trying to decide if it was worth it to go in now and get the job done then and there, or wait and come back with more men of his own to ensure the job was done.

While the knight had his thoughts, I felt indifferent to the outcome to the story at the time. I couldn't have cared less about the people and their precious Magna Carta. If it was destroyed, so be it. It did not concern me. For me, this was just something to watch besides people getting down on their knees and praying all the time.

Finally, the moron walked away and towards the great doors. He left the cathedral that day, but I could sense that he intended on coming back in five days time during the night. And when he would be done with his mission here, the Carta would be burned and erased from history.

Chapter 4: 1215, Continued

The next day, I saw Nathan. I went up to him and could tell he was praying, or meditating. I couldn't tell, but he certainly wanted some privacy.

Me: Wake up!
Nathan: Curse you, Imp.
Me: You've already done that. Guess what Nathan?

Nathan: It's Nathaniel you filth.
Me: That's too formal. You need to relax some Nathan.
Nathan: Hmmph.
Me: So guess what?
Nathan: Can't you just tell me?
Me: I know something you don't.
Nathan: I'm sure. But in the end, you know nothing.
Me: Do you talk this way with everyone?
Nathan: Please just tell me so that you can go away.
Me: That king guy is going to destroy the Carta.
Nathan (opened his eyes): You're lying.
Me: Nope. Swear to Satan. That knight that came here yesterday was ordered by the king to destroy it. He'll be back in four days.
Nathan: A lie, but an interesting lie. Now, please go and leave me be.
Me: Fine! But you'll see.

I had left it at that, and waited for the knight to come back. What else was I going to do? Finally, four days later, at night, the knight came in with four other men. All of them were armed with weapons and held a torch to see. They made their way to the Bishop's office. Three of them, including the knight, went in and shut the door. The other two stood outside of the office to keep watch.

I could not wait to see them come out with the Carta in their hands and destroy it. I hoped that they would do it here. I love a good burning of something important, not to mention that it would cause chaos in the world. I love chaos even more than a good burning.

However, after some time the three came out and I knew instantly they hadn't found it. They were upset, as was I, and they decided to go to the Bishop and threaten his life. What did I care? If the Bishop died, he died. The church would replace him. They always do. I crawled from my pillar and went to the part of the cathedral where his quarters were and waited.

And, oh what a sight to behold. There in the quarters were twelve armed men, waiting for the knight and his men. They were hidden behind the doors, behind the curtains, behind the bookshelves, and wherever else there was a space to hide. The second the last of the knight's men came into the room, the door was closed behind them. Torches and candles were lit all around, and there, surrounding the men who had meant to threaten and probably kill the Bishop, were some nobles and their strongest men, ready to end them.

Immediately, crossbows were fired. Three of the knight's men went down instantly. One was shot in the head, the other in the heart, and the other had three bolts in him so he was certainly done for. The nobles' men rushed at the knight and his last companion, and it was a slaughter. Oh how I laughed and clapped at the violence that ensued that night. For the first time, I did not mind seeing the humans and their petty little lives.

The knight's last man was chopped in half by an axe. Beautiful sight let me tell you. And the knight was down on one knee, sword still in hand, but out of breath and clearly defeated.

Suddenly, Nathan appeared beside me and scared the crap out of me. He did not say anything and merely looked down at the scene down below us.

Me: What the hell are you doing here?
Nathan: I came to make sure the Carta was safe.
Me: Wait. You believed me?
Nathan: Don't look too much into it. I decided to play it safe. I appeared in the Bishop's dreams a few nights ago and warned him.
Me: Any chance you can teach me how to do that? I would -
Nathan: No. Anyway, the Bishop asked the nobles to come and stop the destruction of the Carta. They obliged without hesitation.

Me: Well, well. Nathan, you didn't strike me as the caring type. Not bad for an angel.

Nathan did not reply to that, but I think I saw the smallest bit of a smile. I looked back down and saw the Bishop come out of a side room, holding the Carta. That old Hugh. He did not look pleased at the death in his room, but he nodded to the noblemen and thanked them. The knight looked as if he was about to say something. I sensed that he was going to ask for forgiveness. He was even willing to betray the king if he was allowed to live. But before he could say anything, the Bishop made a signal with his hand, and right away a man with a great, big sword stepped up and cut the knight's head off. The knight's head rolled a few feet towards the door, the Bishop turned and walked away, holding the protected Magna Carta, and that was that.

Chapter 5: Battle of Lincoln's Fair, 1217

Well I tell ya that King John was a big pain for England during his reign. Even after his reign he was still causing trouble. Personally I liked his style. The guy was hated so much by the people though that a civil war started, called the First Barons' War. King John upset the barons so much that they invited a Frenchman to come to England and become the king, some guy named Louis. When John died, his nine year old son, Henry III became king, but a regent was named for him to help rule. That man was William Marshal. Now Marshal was old, nearly seventy, but the man was a knight and had experience, so I suppose that's why he was chosen.

When Marshal took control of the war for Henry, Louis basically had control of the southern half of England. It sure didn't look great for the Royalists (the guys fighting for Henry). As it turned out, the city of Lincoln was still under the control of the Royalists. The Frenchman, Louis, sent an army to capture the castle here and take over. So there was a siege going on. Not a fun time. For the humans that is. As long as they didn't destroy the cathedral I was in the clear. I'm made out of stone. So the lack of food did not bother me, as I don't need it to survive.

Let me correct myself. I can enjoy a delicious meal and a wonderful glass of wine should I desire it. But I do not need it. If a medium rare steak is left on the table, that bad boy is going to disappear. When a bottle of Merlot or Zinfandel is down in the wine cellar, it will be found empty hours later. I've gotten quite a few priests, altar boys, and others in trouble for stealing the good stuff. But hey! I'm only taking what is owed to me. I have been turned into stone for eternity.

Now for the good stuff. Marshal sent an army to Lincoln to end the siege. The nice thing for me was that the cathedral and the castle are right next to each other, and some of the battle happened right here outside of the church. I had the perfect view of the entire thing.

May 20th, 1217. I'll never forget it. All of the sudden, bowmen appeared up on the castle walls and started reigning arrows down into the French army. Men were going down like flies. Poor little Frenchmen. Some of them would occasionally peer up from behind their shields, and one of them would be sure to get an arrow right in the face. What the French army did not know was that this bombardment of arrows was actually meant to be a distraction. While this was going on, the English army under Marshal went around the castle and came into the city from the north.

All of the sudden, the English army came swooping into the city and began attacking the Frenchmen. I saw the terror on their faces as they faced death. Those English soldiers were determined, and led by a pretty wise man. I couldn't help but root for the Royalists. I mean, they're English right? And I'm a stone gargoyle stuck to some pillar in an English cathedral. So it just made sense that I rooted for those guys back in 1217. There I was, jumping up and down, warning a man or two about a Frenchman who was about to chop them down. They couldn't hear me, but I was in the moment. Some of the English men survived the battle, others weren't so lucky.

Now Nathan doesn't know about this, on account that I'm not to ever interfere with events or interact with the humans. But I suddenly sensed that someone intended to kill William Marshal. Marshal was not in the crowd of death and blood, but he stood back at the northern entrance, watching the battle unfold and occasionally giving orders to men around him. I looked over to the side of the cathedral and noticed a man was aiming his bow at the English commander. I couldn't help myself!

Without thinking, I took a pretty hefty stone from the roof and dropped it down on the bowman's head. He died quickly, and Marshal survived. Nathan would have destroyed me if he had found out, but some part of me felt it was necessary to drop that stone. Not to mention I got to be a part of the battle!

As time went on, the French began retreating back into the walls which surrounded the cathedral. Now I really had quite the view. The battle was growing more and more intense. Men lie on the ground, moaning in pain, while others laid motionless, already dead. Some were in Heaven, some were in Hell. I'm not really supposed to get into the details about how that all works. I suppose as an imp I'm really just meant to wreak havoc on Earth and make people miserable, but trust me when I say that once a person goes to the beyond, I pretty much know where they're going. But enough of the religious talk, back to the battle.

As the battle raged in and out of the cathedral close, it began to look as if the French might be able to drive the English back and win this thing. The bowmen that had been on top of the castle were either out of range or out of arrows. The English knights who had been fighting were getting tired, and bodies lay everywhere. I was no longer enjoying the mayhem and death, and just wanted this scene to end. That's when the idea hit me.

Me: Nathan! Where are you? Come out and help!
Nothing.
Me: Nathan?

Nathan was nowhere to be found.

Chapter 6: Battle of Lincoln's Fair, Continued

The battle was at a stand still. Men were dying all around the castle and the cathedral and there was nothing I could do about except watch. I called out for

Nathan but he would not answer. I scurried my way over the stones and pillars on my way to the altar, where Nathan typically liked to rest. I checked the altar, but he wasn't there. I did not dare touch the Bible that lay there, so I tried tossing a few things at it to see if a nudge or two would wake the guy up. No stones I can tell you that. Little stuff like a candle or pendant. After a few attempts, nothing. No Nathan. The angel was either in a deep sleep that would not be disturbed, or he was not there.

I crawled my way up the side of the building and went up to the tip top of the cathedral, hoping that maybe he was praying. Nothing. No angel or even a pigeon. I figured at least that if he was outside somewhere I could see him from the very top there. And I was right. There he was, walking around the cloister, a beautiful relaxing spot for people to wander and gather their thoughts. Though not where I figured anyone would be while there was a battle raging.

I raced down as fast as I could, and I got there panting and out of breath. Just kidding I don't need air. But I was in a hurry and wanted to emphasize how quickly I was moving about.

The cloister is a beautiful little area as I said before. Today, in the present day, there is a cafe where food is available for people who come to tour the cathedral. You can also walk around and smell the stone and imagine all of the history that has taken place here. Imagine a small yard, surrounded by covered hallways with pillars all around. People can sit and enjoy the peacefulness of it all. One of my favorite things to do is go and grab a cup of warm, hazelnut coffee when no one is looking, and just hold it in my hands and take the occasional sip as I look around the cloister and up at the cathedral's towers. I especially love it on a cool day, so that the coffee warms up my stone cold hands. Rain or shine, there's somewhere to sit and take it all in…

Oh crap I got off topic. Anyway, there was Nathan strolling around the cloister, hands behind his back, eyes closed. He must have counted the steps before or have super vision because he knew exactly when to turn at the next corner. He walked around those halls so gracefully, it was as if he was… well, an angel. I could not help myself but watch him walk before I could say anything.

Those angels got the good end of the bargain. Nathan has very nice dark blond hair, with some curl to it, and is about shoulder length. He has flawless skin, the color of a peach. The man was certainly tall to me, but he seemed tall for any species to be honest. I'd say he is about six foot two. He is your typical angel with the clothing, wearing a white flowy robe that just brushes the ground at the bottom, as if it was trying to very lightly sweep away all the bad things in the world.

I felt myself come out of the
trance, remembering the battle
going on right outside the walls,
and went over to Nathan.

Nathan: There is nothing I can do.
Me: What? How'd you know?
Nathan: I just had a feeling you
were going to ask.
Me: Well why can't you do
anything?
Nathan: It is not our way.
Me: What the hell does that mean?
Nathan: The Lord believes in free
will, and war is evil, so we are
not to interfere with the humans
when they are in a battle.
Me: You gotta be kidding me! You
appeared in the Bishop's dream a
few years ago. Wasn't that
interfering?
Nathan: The Bishop did not have
ill intentions, nor was it war. By
sending a message a critical piece
of history was saved for the
humans.
Me: Seems to me there's some grey
area there. So you're just going
to watch the humans die?

Nathan: I am not going to watch. I am here, .walking and praying for them all.
Me: What kind of crap is that? I thought you "loved" humans and all that?
Nathan: I do. It pains me to not be able to stop it and save them all. But it is not possible. Sometimes all we can do when we love someone is wait for their mistake to be made and comfort them in whatever way we can.
Me: Whatever angel boy. I'm out of here.

As I went back up to the top of the tower to watch the action, the battle was becoming a struggle for both sides. Men continued to throw their shields in front of them as swords and spears came crashing down. Arrows occasionally were being loosed into crowds of soldiers, and every once in a while finding their mark, resulting in a man writhing on the ground, or instant death. Behind the fighting warriors, there stood commanders screaming orders, encouraging their men to push forward and turn the battle in their favor. I could see that they were trying to be brave and convince their men of victory, but what I saw in their eyes was fear. They were afraid of losing the battle at any moment, but deep down they were terrified that they were going to die. These men were not ready for death. They were not ready for their Heaven. They wished to live. Humans. So predictable.

Suddenly I sensed it. Courage. A determination not to live, but to be victorious. To be a hero. To be remembered. Many humans want to be remembered and honored, but only a few follow this desire and risk everything for it. This man was risking it. He no longer cared if he lived or died that day. Then I saw him. A royalist Knight running through the masses and heading right towards the commander of the French army.

Surely the man couldn't survive this suicidal charge. But

it was as if luck, or God, was
protecting him. Arrows flew past
his head by mere inches, swords
that swung at him could not find
their mark, and shields were
apparently as light as the wind as
he pushed them aside. I later
found out the knight went by the
name of Reginald Croc.

So Reg arrived to where the
French commander stood, whom I
believe was a Count. And this
Count was wearing armor, making it
difficult to find a weak area to
strike and bring him down. Does
that stop ole Reg? Nope. He lunges
forward, rolls underneath a
swinging death blow by the Count,
and thrusts his sword in between
two armor plates and into the
Count's side. The Count gasped,
his eyes widened, and after
stuttering some measely words,
fell to the ground, dead as a
doornail.

I sensed where his soul was
going, and I had this odd feeling.
I don't know why. Nathan's words
rung in my head, as if the
cathedral's bells were going off.

Pray. Love. Comfort. I heard those words and then saw the men dying in battle. It was weird. I shook myself out of it, my attention coming back to the battle.

Those around the Count had started panicking. They lacked the courage to take his place and try to turn the battle around in their favor. Their priority was living, not victory. One of them began yelling retreat to all of the French soldiers. With that, the French fled faster than a dog getting beat by his master. They no longer had any battle tactics, no longer were they in formation to protect one another. The English chased after them. Taking down any who fell behind. Another English force came from nowhere and also began killing the fleeing Frenchmen. It was becoming a rout. A slaughter almost. The French were gone. The siege of Lincoln was done.

I started cheering. The English humans had won the battle. I don't know why I felt like cheering. I couldn't tell if it was because the English had won or if the battle was over.

The battle wasn't over just yet however. The English began looting some of the homes and shops in the town. Glass shattered as windows were broken. Wood cracked as doors were kicked or battered down by soldiers. Screams were heard all over. This I grew angry at. If anyone was going to mess with the people of Lincoln, it was going to be me! If I'm going to be cast into stone and be cursed here in this town forever, it's going to be my town. It was then in 1217 that I decided that. I screamed down at the English soldiers committing the looting, cursing their names. They couldn't hear me of course, but it made me feel better.

Suddenly, I heard weeping down below, back near the cloister. I found my way over there and saw Nathan, crouched down next to some men who were lying on the ground. Some laid there moaning or crying for their mothers, death on its way to take

them. Others lay motionless,
having already been visited by
Grim.

The one that Nathan was
crouched next to was near death's
door, but was not crying or
moaning. His eyes were open, and
he was looking up, almost as if he
was trying to see the birds in the
clouds and pinpoint each
individual feather's color. But it
was not the clouds, or the birds,
he was looking at. It was the
heavens. I realized this because
the man was praying. I flinched at
his words, hearing words like God,
love, Christ, forgiveness, etc.

Nathan's hand was laid on the
man's shoulder throughout all of
this. He was praying with the man,
offering words of comfort. Just
like he said he would. As the
man's eyes began to close for the
last time, Nathan gave his
shoulder a reassuring squeeze. I
saw the man's soul leave and go
up, up into those clouds above,
and beyond. When I looked back at
Nathan, he was standing, looking
at all the dead men lying on this

sacred ground of his, and a tear
gently leaving his cheek. He
glanced my way for an instant,
gave the briefest of nods, and
turned away. I decided it would be
wise to give him some space.

I had many emotions then. Too
many to explain and they're my
business, so let's just leave it
at that.

Chapter 7: President Day, Continued

A few days went by, about a
week away from Christmas Day, when
I saw her again. And again, she
came into the cathedral crying and
bruised. This time however, she
went to a corner where candles
could be lit, and prayed. She
prayed in a whisper, but I sat
above her and with my excellent
hearing could hear her
conversation with God.

She asked God why her father
hit her and threw things at her
whenever he grew angry or became
drunk. She wondered if it was
really her fault that her mother

died when she was born like her father said. She asked for God's forgiveness and wished that her mother could be alive so that her daddy would love her. She began to cry again, not wanting to go back home, but eventually convinced herself it was in her best interest to return before her father grew angry for her being out so late.

For days I pondered what I had seen and heard. I felt sorry for the girl. I grew angry at the thought of her father punishing her for something that was beyond her control. I wanted him dead. I wanted HIM punished.

I tried not to let it ruin my holidays. At times I'd watch a good Christmas film like Home Alone or Die Hard as I enjoyed a cup of peppermint coffee. And in the afternoons and evenings I poured my heart out as I watched the football club win another match. The days flew by and I realized it was Christmas Eve. The season had gone too quickly as always, but that is life. Even though I am thousands of years old, time can fly by at times.

Anyway, the day began very nicely and I allowed myself one more day to binge Christmas movies and play Christmas songs on my old record player. Bing Crosby's "White Christmas" as it snows outside really is a delight. Suddenly, as Bing was wishing that all my Christmases be white, I heard her again. The girl. I hadn't noticed her come into the cathedral this time. She was crying at her usual spot. I immediately stopped the record player and crawled my way over to where she sat.

When I saw her I was shocked. Her lip was bloodied and she had a black eye. She was trembling, whether from fright or pain I wasn't sure. It was obvious what had happened, but I still felt surprise overcome me, followed by anger. I couldn't believe her father had done this to her. This poor child.

She wasn't sure what to do. The uncertainty of not knowing

where she could go and where she
would be safe was terrifying, and
it is wretched that a child ever
has to go through this kind of
traumatic situation in life. She
cried aloud that she had nowhere
to go, but was too terrified to go
back, worried what the monster
would do to her upon her return.

I had a thought, and then
hesitated. I wasn't sure how much
I could do. I am strictly
forbidden from interacting with
the humans and making my
circumstances known to them. I
shrugged and came up with a
solution. I ran back to the
kitchen and gathered some food and
drink. Not alcoholic of course. I
made some hot chocolate and
grabbed a few croissants for her.

I ran back to the pews as
fast as I could, hoping the poor
thing had not left already. I was
practically begging for her to be
there. I almost felt the urge to
say a prayer to the Big Guy.
(Sorry I almost threw up typing
that.)

I came into the church and was devastated not to see her. I went to one of the glass stained windows, where a beautiful design was, but I had no time to appreciate its beauty and artistry. I peered through the glass, hoping I could see her just leaving and maybe stop her in some way, so that she would be back in the church safe and sound. But no luck.

Then I heard the soft whimper. I went back toward the pews and found lying on one of them, farther away from the great doors of the cathedral. She lay there shivering and crying ever so softly, trying her best to stay warm with only the clothes she wore.

I pondered for a moment, considering how I should play this, when the idea came to me. I put the food and hot chocolate on the pew behind her, gave a knock on the wood, and scurried away. The girl had been startled, rightly so of course. But after her fear began to drift away and she looked over the pew, she saw the food and drink. She looked around, wondering who could have possibly left this for her, but seeing no one, slowly went and began to eat. She was starving, and ate the croissants like a starving predator in the wild. She then carefully sipped the hot chocolate, and when the sweet sugar hit her taste buds, the smallest and cutest smile revealed itself. She held the cup in her hands, enjoying not just the taste of the chocolatey goodness, but the warmth it provided as well.

That led me to my next idea. I ran back to the kitchen, got the fireplace going, set up some blankets and a pillow into an acceptable bed, and then set up the record player. I figured music would be the best way to possibly entice the child to come this way and find the bed and the fire. As much as I didn't want to, I chose "Here Comes Santa Claus" by Gene Autry because I figured a child would like hearing the famous fat man's name on Christmas Eve.

I started the record player and headed back to the girl, who had finished her drink and sat there, wondering what she should do next. When she first heard the music, she immediately crouched down behind the pew, carefully glancing to see if someone was there. Upon seeing no one, she hesitantly started to walk towards the sound. When she reached the kitchen, she walked in and looked around to see who was there, cooking or cleaning dishes possibly, but there was no one. She saw some more food (some blueberry muffins) and more hot chocolate by the quickly made bed, and walked over to it. There, next to the food, laid a note which said, "Enjoy and stay the night if you'd like. Happy Christmas."

The girl read the note aloud and then seemed a little startled by it all. I can't say I blamed her for feeling that way. Trust is something that she would probably struggle with her entire life. She began walking away from the bed, and I could sense that she meant

to run. I didn't know what to do.
I felt that there was no way she
could go back to that brute. The
poor child needed help, and I
wanted to give her that.

She began to turn away, and I
panicked. I knew she would feel
like there was nothing else she
could do but go back. The note
wasn't going to do the trick. What
else was I going to do? The girl
needed someone to finally watch
out for her, so as she reached the
kitchen door and began to open it,
I broke the rule.

"Stop."

Chapter 8: High in the Sky, 1311

Since the Battle of Lincoln's
Fair, the town had become bigger
and more influential in England.
The cathedral was known throughout
the country as it continued to
expand. There was a time when
Lincoln Cathedral was the tallest
building in the world you know.
Taller than the pyramids even. The
central spire reached a height of
525 feet. I counted it myself to

be sure. I still remember the day
it was completed.

    This cathedral that has been
my home for hundreds of years now
is a sight to behold. When the sun
rises, the light hits the stone
architecture and stained glass
windows in such a way it makes you
want to stare at it all day long.
The figures in the windows dance
as the sun rises and sets. I've
almost felt like they were alive
and wanted to talk with me as I
enjoyed my morning cup of coffee.
At night, the towers hover above
you in the night sky, not in a
menacing way, far from it. But in
a way that makes you feel secure,
protected almost. Those two iconic
towers are not just a part of
Lincoln, they are a symbol for it.

    The men of Lincoln had been
working hard on this masterpiece,
and boy did they work. There's not
much to tell really when it comes
to the completion of this
magnificent feat, but there is a
story I do wish to share before my
time as a stone imp has come to an
end.

Being a part of the architecture means I hear and see everything that goes on up in the towers and on the roof of the cathedral. I remember that as they were getting close to finishing the spire and being able to observe their masterpiece, there was an accident. One of the men, John, I believe his name was, was at the top of the central spire, when the wooden boards beneath him fell apart. Before John's fall, I overheard him talking to one of his workmates:

John: Bloody hell I'm tired.
Workmate: Almost done with this now John. Fancy a drink after we're done?
John: I wish I could. Got to get home to the wife and kids. I miss the little tramps.
Workmate: Always going home to the little ones. Must love your life.
John: It doesn't matter if I'm rich or not, as long as I have those kids and they have me all is well.

Workmate: How do you find the time
of day to work and be the father?
John: Well, it's not -

    Down, down, down John fell.
Now I've studied Newton's laws of
gravity, but when I look back and
think about John's fall, time
seemed to stop. John was slowly
falling to the ground, screaming,
knowing his death was inevitable.
As he was falling, I couldn't help
but think about what he was just
saying. You know, about his kids.
I don't have kids, but I sure
could tell that man loved his.
Remember, I have this sort of
gift. As people are near death, I
feel something within them. I know
who they are, their life, and
what's in store for them in the
afterlife. John was a good man. He
was going to Heaven. It just
didn't seem fair to let this guy
die and leave his kids all alone.
    That being said, I helped him
out a little. Just a teensy bit
mind you. Now an imp is not that
strong, being so small and
everything. But since I've turned

to stone that's all changed. So as John fell and was close to the end, he caught something. My stone foot. I had sat down on a pillar, crossed my right leg over the other, and my left leg stuck out just enough for an object falling down the side of the cathedral to catch hold. In this case that object was John. It hurt. The man had to weigh almost ninety kilograms.

John hung there from my foot, screaming for a moment. Then he slowly began to realize that he wasn't dying. He began sobbing. In a good way. He began thanking God and looking up to Heaven. I was tempted to drop him for that, but I held back from the temptation. He looked at me eventually and thanked God again. Then he patted me on the side over and over, grateful that I was there on the side of the cathedral.

His buddies came over to get him down. They were shocked that John was alive. Some were even cheering, patting him on the back. John was relieved. He was allowed to go home for the day. As he began walking away from the others on his way home, I noticed him stop in the middle of the road, turn to look back at the cathedral, and give a nod directly at me. There was a brief second where I thought he knew my secret, but then I realized he was just silently thanking this stone imp that happened to be there on the side of the most beautiful and tallest cathedral in the world.

P.S. - Nathan isn't allowed to know about that.

Chapter 9: The Plague, 1300's

_____The sins of man are too great for this world to bear. That's what the bishop said to the people of Lincoln anyway. As the plague, or Black Death, spread throughout the continent like an unstoppable storm, people began to die a horrible death. Fevers and headaches made people cry out in pain and pray to God for mercy. The chills these poor souls experienced made you think they were living out in the cold tundras of the north, and as if a cocoon of ice was forming around their entire bodies. And then when things couldn't seem any worse, there were the nodes, or buboes. These painful lumps covered their bodies and were extremely painful. There was no way to lie down or sit comfortably. Doctors believed that popping them would help the evil spirits leave the bodies of these sinners. But it was not the answer. Nothing was.

You should have seen all of the ways people tried to "remove" the plague. First there was the killing of all the cats and dogs, as some believed they were the ones passing on the plague to humans. Then there was the plucking of chickens. Some believed that this practice would somehow drag the evil out of their own body and into the chicken's. Absurd. And then of course, the deeply religious ones came through the town and preached of God's wrath being brought down on the

Earth for people's sins. Some went even so far as to whip themselves, as if punishing themself would absolve them of their sin and the plague would just go away. Poor humans.

What's even worse was the fact that at first, many did not believe the plague was a real thing. It was all made up. It was a tale that the poor were passing on from town to town to spice up their lives and put fear into the children and God-fearing souls of the land. As a result, many people went about their lives, and by the time they accepted the reality, it was too late. The plague had come, and it had spread. It spread amongst the population like a wildfire, and nothing would stop it. Hell had come to England.

Throughout the night, people cried out in pain. Whether it was from their own pain or the pain of losing someone they loved, I could not tell. Death was at our door, and he was busy every day and every night. Bodies lined the streets and people came pouring into the cathedral, begging for forgiveness, food, or a solution. Sometimes they asked for all three. It was chaos. At first I thought I loved it, but as time went on and I saw the misery that people were facing, I came to loathe it. I felt pity for the humans.

The Bishop stayed clear of the people as often as he could. He stayed in his quarters. He claimed it was to pray for the souls of the people and study the Bible for answers, but he just wanted to stay away from anyone who might be affected. There were priests, monks, and nuns who would directly help the people. One such nun, Agnes, was in and around the cathedral often. One note here: yes, Agnes was a common name, especially for a nun, but whether it was the name given to her by her parents, or a name she chose upon becoming a nun, the name was a perfect fit for her. Agnes means "pure," and this woman was indeed pure. She was kind, loving, and comforting to all of those around

her. Whether they were sick or
healthy, wealthy or poor, Agnes
took care of them.

Each and every day, Agnes
came and welcomed the sick and the
depressed. As time went on, I
found myself following her and
enjoyed watching her kindness take
on many forms. She would hold a
child who cried over their dead
mother or father, sometimes both.
She would feed a man who was
unable to lift his hand or could
barely open his lips. She prayed
with those who were near death,
and held their hand as they
slipped away into the darkness. I
began to have feelings for this
woman, a human nonetheless. And a
kind one at that! She was
certainly very beautiful, with
blonde hair that occasionally
slipped out from underneath her
white cap that all the nuns wore.
But it was not her beauty that
made me love her. No. In fact, I
rarely thought of that. It was her
kindness and love for all. It made
me think that perhaps, in a
perfect world, she could even love

me and care for me. But alas, a nun and an imp could never be together. And I sadly accepted this.

I came so close to talking to her once. She was alone, gathering some food from the kitchen for the sick. I watched from above and so badly wanted to go and talk to her. I wanted to say such nice and wonderful things to her. To compliment her on her generosity, to tell her I wish I was capable of showing kindness to others as she did, and to tell her I longed for a life where the two of us could be with one another. At that time in my life, I was still very uncertain about how far I could get with breaking the rules. I feared that if I did speak to a human, my life would immediately come to an end, and I would be stone for all of eternity.

As I began to crawl away from my hiding place in the kitchen, I slipped and made a loud bagning sound. Agnes heard it and immediately turned in my direction. There was no fear in her eyes. She turned, as if she was expecting some poor soul to be wandering in and asking for food. She showed surprise when there was no one there, and looked around the kitchen. As I sat deep in the shadows in one of the corners, she turned and without realizing it she looked right into my eyes. I felt something inside of me burst when her wonderful blue eyes looked into mine. She smiled as went back to her work. For a second, I thought she had smiled at me, but I then realized she had smiled because that's just who she was. I have rarely acknowledged it since, but I knew then that from my part, it was love.

I do not know whether love can be eternal or ends when one's life comes to a stop. I feel that I have loved Agnes to this day, even though she died during the plague. Her love and kindness to all others eventually gave her the sickness, and just a few days later, she passed. Even in her pain and suffering, her beauty and warmth had remained.

I felt her soul immediately go to Heaven, and I swear the angels all gathered round and welcomed her with open arms. I went to the roof of the cathedral to look at the heavens, and the sun was setting with a most marvelous glow across the land. The skies showed a variety of colors that were gorgeous and mesmerizing. I would say I fondly remember the color pink when I think of that day. It was a sad day, but for me it was probably the most memorable day of my measly life. And as I sat there and watched the sun depart, I smiled to myself and whispered, "Agnes."

Chapter 10: Henry VIII, 1541

You know a lot of people give King Henry VIII a hard time. I always thought of him as a genius in some ways! Anyone with a basic knowledge of world history knows about the English Reformation and how Henry separated the country from the Catholic Church. The guy wants a new wife, so he has to divorce his current wife. But the Pope won't let him. So what does he do? He creates a new Church of England and bam! Problem solved. He then ordered that all of England convert to this church. Those were some crazy times let me tell you. Catholics became Anglicans all of the sudden. Some Catholics refused to become Anglicans. And some Catholics said they were Anglicans but were actually still Catholics.

Years later, after this official conversion of England, King Henry came to Lincoln as he progressed northward through the country, almost like a tour. He was welcomed to the city and praised by his subjects who lined the streets. It was a perfect day for it. The sun shone brightly, just a few clouds in the sky, a slight breeze to cool the people on that warm day. Men, women, and children were cheering and waving, dying to see their King.

I saw him as he neared the cathedral. He was a large man by

this time in his life. He was imposing and clearly demanded respect and attention by all those around him. He had a few years left to live, but the man certainly lived like a king. He had a reddish, brown beard, a chubby face, and wore very fancy regal clothes. I find clothes restricting so I'm not much into that look. I like to imagine if I was human that I'd wear sweatpants or jeans all day, with a comfortable sweater. But that's just me.

He came inside the cathedral, got a tour, had the bishop kiss his hand, went up to the altar and crossed himself, and then left to be taken to his sleeping quarters for the night.

As I was about to head to a nice spot to enjoy some red wine for the afternoon, something caught my attention. There she was. A young woman, clearly royalty, who came into the cathedral happy and giggling. She did not seem to have a care in the world, and enjoyed laughing. I saw the woman twirl around to take everything in, then dash up to the altar. Her ladies-in-waiting tried to keep up with her, but were failing miserably. This was indeed the young Queen Catherine Howard, the fifth wife of our dear Henry VIII.

I found my interest piqued, so I stuck around. It turned out to be worth it, because not long after the Queen ordered her ladies away, saying she wished to pray. She knelt down for a few minutes, and then he came. A young man, older than the Queen, but still young. He was thin, had dark brown hair, and pale skin. He went up behind her, put his hands through her hair, and then pulled her head back to kiss him. The Queen smiled. I was intrigued now more than ever and listened to their conversation:

Queen: Thomas Culpepper, you naughty boy.
Thomas: Your Majesty, I apologize. Did I overstep?

Queen: Of course not, my love.
I've missed you.
Thomas: I miss you too Catherine.
This whole trip through England
has been nothing but misery. I
miss being able to rendezvous with
you back in London.
Queen: I know darling. Soon we
will be back and all will be
right.

The two continued kissing,
passionately. That Culpepper
decided to get some too. They went
over to one of the alcoves on the
side of the church and he held her
up against the wall. From there
all it took was hiking up the
Queen's dress a little. I enjoyed
the show while it lasted, really
wishing that I had that glass of
wine with me as I sat back and
watched. You don't get to see that
kind of stuff in church.
As those two were
consummating their love, I noticed
a noble woman coming into the
church and walking in their
direction. Now things were going
to get more interesting! I was

ecstatic. A little drama to add to the scene. I could've found a way to stop those two, but I decided to stay out of it this time. I had gotten bored the last couple hundred years. Some new drama was appreciated.

Just as the two lovers finished and were in the middle of making sure their clothes were on just right, the noble woman came across them and gasped. I almost laughed aloud. It was too funny.

The Queen could have handled the situation with regal authority if she had chosen to, but the poor young woman who was in love did not take control when she had the chance. Culpepper awkwardly excused himself from the ladies and walked off in a hurry. He was practically running out by the time he got to the church doors.

The Queen muttered some things about praying and something being wrong with her dress. She went back to the altar, knelt down, and prayed. The noble woman, after seeing the Queen had nothing else to say, turned and walked out. She had a smile on her lips, and it was clear she now had something she could hold over the young queen. When I saw that smile, it was then that I realized the Queen's life was ruined. I felt a little bad about that. Perhaps I should have done something to help those two, but I just wanted to enjoy the moment and have a good laugh.

It turned out that the affair came to be known by many close to the King. Henry ordered Thomas Culpepper to be beheaded, and his head was placed on London Bridge for everyone to see. The poor Queen was beheaded as well. I don't know why, but I felt her death when it happened. I felt the fear in her heart screaming up until the last second, when I assume an axe or sword came down to finish the short life she had. At least when she died, she went to Heaven.

I talked to Nathan about it later. I hadn't talked to him in awhile and was curious.

Me: So the Queen was beheaded today.
Nathan: True.
Me: What for?
Nathan: Adultery.
Me: What? Just because she had sex with a guy?
Nathan: It is a sin.
Me: And the King doesn't sin?
Nathan: Well, yes, but that's different.
Me: How the hell is that different?
Nathan (looks at me disapprovingly for swearing): He is the King. And while yes, it is a shame that he fornicates with other women, he is the head of the church.
Me: Sounds like there's a double standard.
Nathan: What's your point, imp?
Me: That life sucks, but it sounds like it really sucks to be a woman in this life.

Chapter 11: The 1600's & 1700's

Humans, if there is anything that I've discovered observing you from close and afar, it is that

life is hard. There are times
when I've envied you and your
lives, and there are times when I
have not. It goes without saying
that an imp turned to stone is not
the ideal life. And yet I've seen
you quiver in fear, pray for your
cures, cry in the night, and beg
for something better.

In the seventeenth century,
some of you finally began to try
and do something about that. You
left your homes, went to the
coast, boarded a ship, and went
off to the Americas. To the new
world. A new beginning.

In the 1640's I believe,
right outside the cathedral, a
young man ran up to an older man,
his father it turns out, to ask
why he'd done what he'd done. He
screamed and lashed out at his
father, demanding an answer. The
man took it. He didn't reply. He
let his son, a teenager, hit him,
scream at him, and threaten him.
Eventually, the son fell to his
knees, head down, and cried. His
father sat down next to him,
hugged him, and cried as well. The

two of them sat there, on the
ground, in broad daylight, rocking
back and forth and consoling one
another. It turned out that the
father, who could not afford to
care for his son properly any
longer, had agreed for him to
become an indentured servant in
the Virginia colony. His father
was not proud of it, nor was he
happy about it. In fact he dreaded
it, hated himself for agreeing to
it, and would miss his son very
much. He begged his son for
forgiveness and told him that he
hoped for him to have a long,
healthy, successful life. He had
hopes that his son would one day
be a wealthy landowner, or have
some type of trade that would
allow him to live comfortably,
with a beautiful wife and
children. The father sobbed when
he thought of the fact he would
probably never see his son, nor
ever see his grandchildren.
        There was nothing I could do
for some of this lot. I asked
Nathan once or twice, but he said
something about free will and all

that. And that struggle was a necessary part of life that humans could and would overcome when they set their minds to it. I argued with him then, just to argue with him honestly, but I suppose there is a bit of truth in what he said.

People were struggling, barely getting by, poor souls who hated their lives and even more depressing, themselves. I once saw a woman, with an old dress that was dirty and had certainly seen better days, come into the cathedral one day, go as close to the altar as she dared and began to cry.

She did not know how to feed herself and her starving children. I looked into her soul and felt something I haven't ever in another person. Pure selflessness. Pure love. It was warm, like hugging a loaf of bread right out of the oven. I could feel the love she had for her children. She would do anything for them. I could sense it. She lived and breathed for these children. Every heartbeat was for the sole purpose of keeping those children and making their lives better. Her husband was no more and she was praying to God. She asked him for forgiveness, for the things she was thinking about doing to provide for her children. She asked him for guidance, seeking another route. She asked aloud if perhaps there was a way to get to the New World and take care of them there. But she cried because that was impossible, given the circumstances. No one would take her as an indentured servant. Nor was there any way that she could afford passage across the Atlantic.

    I thought back to the argument that Nathan and I had about the struggles of life. I felt anger rise inside of me, and decided it was not necessary for this mother to struggle. If anything, her children especially did not NEED to struggle any longer, as they're children and have no control over such things. I saw their faces through the mother's tears and that was it. A

little girl, the age of three or
four, and a big brother, probably
about seven or eight years old.

I moved along the walls and
passageways of the cathedral,
making certain that no one noticed
me, and found my hoard of goods,
trinkets, and such. I'm not going
to reveal the location of this
stash in case you're wondering.
You'd have to find that yourself
if you're ever willing to look. I
rummaged through it all and
finally found my stash of coins. I
had quite a lot of money stashed
away. I'm not particularly proud
of this, but I'd found money… in
the offering bowls after a
service. I'd also taken a coin or
two from the Bishop's quarters.
And not to mention people left
money around all the time. So
needless to say, I was saving up
money pretty well.

I took a small purse heavy
with coin, clutched it in my stone
cold hands, and for the first
time, I almost felt some warmth in
them. Pretty ludicrous for a stone
gargoyle. I wrote something on a

small piece of parchment and then
headed my way back to the church.
She was still there. She had
stopped crying and was in the
process of trying to compose
herself before she left the
cathedral.

I went to the very last pew
of the church, toward the great
doors, and put the purse at the
end of the pew. Back to my hiding
place I went, and watched as she
was heading out. I tensed as I saw
her approach the small purse, and
then began to panic when I saw her
walking past it.

I did the first thing I
thought of and threw a small stone
at the last pew. It ricocheted off
of the pew and made a loud "whack"
kind of sound. The poor woman
turned immediately, frightened and
frantically looking around to see
what had just happened. She then
noticed the purse, looked to see
if anyone else was around that may
have dropped it or left it behind
on accident. Seeing no one, she
picked it up and read the note
that lay next to it. After reading

it, she quickly opened the purse and began to cry. But these were tears of relief and happiness. She looked back at the cross at the front of the church, and thanked God. She ran out of the cathedral, on her way home, to start a new life and care for her children.

Am I a hero? Yes of course. But I knew that I couldn't give myself the credit, so I said on the note that the money was from God. I figured she'd be more willing to take it. What was I going to do with the money anyway? I'm an imp turned to stone stuck in a cathedral for eternity, or until I'm destroyed, whichever comes first.

Here's the note.

Dear Sad Woman,
You are blessed. Take this money and prosper. From, God

P.S. - Bring back a bottle of stout and leave it in this exact spot if able.

Chapter 12: WWI, 1914

Demons love when humans go to war. Death is ever present and humans show their true colors. In 1914, I was thrilled when I heard "the war to end all wars" was beginning. Pride, nationalism, parades, and excitement were everywhere in the town. Men were signing up for the army fast, thirsty for war. Women were crying but they were proud of their men for joining the war effort.

I'll never forget what that war did to the people of this town, this country. So often, women and children came into the church, praying for their husbands, sons, and fathers to come home. Many came to cry after getting the news that those same loved ones they prayed for were gone. I would often bring the war up in conversation with Nate (sometimes I call him Nate to really bother him) to get his take on it and see what the Big Guy upstairs had to say about it all.

Me: So the Big Guy is okay with all of this huh?

Nate: Of course not Imp. We've discussed this before, please don't make me say it yet again.

Me: Alright, alright. Free will. But, this Great War? Really? Seems like something could be done by all the powerful one.

Nate: You're mocking again.

Me: You're right, I am.

Nate: Besides, you enjoy chaos. You enjoy death. You enjoy MISERY.

He had me there. I was a demon, of course I enjoyed these things. But now my town, my people, were miserable and I wasn't the cause of it! I'm selfish that way. I didn't like seeing these men going off and not coming back. I wanted to throw stones at em, trip them up occasionally, or splash them with water from the roof as they walked outside the cathedral. This was different.

I began to realize my inner demon-ness was fading. No, not fading. More like… changing. For hundreds of years I fought this. I want to be the bad guy. The stone imp that causes mayhem and destruction. Sometimes I do, for old times' sake. But I could sense feelings of...ugh I hate typing this down, human. Let's get back to the story.

You know Lincoln became a pretty big part of the war effort. Factories in the city were helping make airplanes and more importantly, Lincoln invented and built the tank. That's right. THE tank. Get inside one of those bad boys and you were riding over trenches in style and staying safe. For the most part. So yeah, the great city of Lincoln became known as "Tank Town."

I still remember seeing the first one. They had it parade through the streets. A way to boost morale and show the people that England was going to win this great big war thanks to their hard work. I watched from the roof of the cathedral as it went by, and I myself felt a slight sense of pride. I was in such good spirits that day I stole a good bottle of Merlot from the Bishop's room. Drank the whole bottle too. I stole a little steak from the kitchen, nice medium rare (when you're stone you don't concern yourself with how you eat) filet mignon, and devoured that while sipping the wine. Great combination right? I bet you're thinking of steak now too.

So anyway, I particularly remember in 1918, the last year of the war, a little love story that took place. There was this young couple, very young. They were both teenagers. The guy might have just turned eighteen. He had been working at the tank factory. Good looking face, dark blonde hair, tall and thin. His name was Timothy. The girl was lovely, with red hair and a few freckles on her white cheeks. Her name was Elizabeth. They had come to the cathedral often to talk and be alone with another.

As I saw them look at one another, it was clear they were in love. Once, he put his hand in her red hair and pulled her close to him. I could see the readiness in their eyes. I could sense the determination to show their love to one another. A passionate heat radiated from the two of them that I even felt. It was something to behold. I came to respect those two. I almost felt myself becoming a guardian for them. I would be a lookout while they were together, and I would never watch them in the act.

One day, Timothy told Elizabeth that he had signed up for the army. She was devastated. She begged him not to go. She begged him to stay. He couldn't do it. He went on about duty (don't know what that is) and how if he didn't fight he would never forgive himself. It was typical for young men at that time to think that way. They felt obligated to fight in a war that they didn't truly understand. They saw war as a chance to leave the homes that they had been stuck in their whole lives. It was an opportunity to go and see the world. To be honored. To have glory. To be remembered.

Timothy told Elizabeth he loved her, he told her they would marry when he returned, he kissed her, and then he left. Elizabeth sobbed for a long while. She prayed for a long while. What made me really remember that day was the song she sang afterward. As she began to walk towards the doors, the sun was setting, causing the stained glass windows to shine brightly. To this, Elizabeth began to sing "Till We Meet Again." It was the most amazing thing I've ever heard in my time here at the cathedral. She sang it slowly, pouring love into every word that echoed off the walls and windows of the church. As she sang the end of the song, she paused at the great doors. "*So wait and pray each night for me, Till we meet again.*" She wiped the tears off her face, opened the doors, and walked out.

Timothy never came back. He died in that war. I think it was at the Battle of Amiens. They say

he died a hero. I felt Elizabeth's
anguish when she came into the
church. She had no more tears by
the time she came to the
cathedral. It was one of those
moments where I wish as her self-
chosen guardian that I could go
and comfort her. But it was
strictly forbidden. I am an imp. A
stone imp.

    I have an old record player
you know. I somehow managed to get
my hands on a record that plays
that song. Every now and then, I
play it when no one is around. I
let it echo off the walls of the
cathedral. I cannot cry, but when
that song plays, I feel as if I
almost could. I don't know why I
play it. I don't know if it's for
Elizabeth, or Timothy, or just for
me. I suppose I like to think that
Timothy hears that song playing
and it reminds him of the love
that he and Elizabeth shared. I
don't sleep. I don't need it. But
I'll find myself closing my eyes
every time I hear the final words
of that song. And when I do, I see
a young Elizabeth, standing at the

doors of the cathedral, happy and in love. Till we meet again.

Chapter 13: WWII

Life seemed to be getting back to normal after that war, until the next one came. It just never seems to end.

In England, when the war began, it was decided that the children should be evacuated to the countryside, away from the cities. Many were sent to Lincolnshire. Occasionally, the families watching them would bring them to Lincoln, and bring them to the cathedral.

I saw those little children, scared and nervous. They were wondering where their mothers and fathers were. Wondering how long it would be before they would see them again.

One little boy, whose name was Arlo, was very sweet. He was only three, with bright blonde hair and a smile that brightened all around him. His evacuee family brought him to the cathedral often. He loved to run around the pews, playing peek-a-boo with anyone who was willing, and loved to play with some toy trucks he had brought with him.

Before my time at the cathedral, children were little humans that were easy to terrify. I loved it. My fellow demons and I would scare children all the time. When one of us imps got a little one to pee or crap himself out of fright, all of the others had to buy drinks for that imp. It was a game of sorts for us that we enjoyed immensely.

Now, however, after spending so much time with humans and coming to understand their misery and grief, I came to somewhat appreciate them and even… care for them. And in 1940 I very much came to appreciate this little boy. A few times, he wandered off from his evacuee family and would play around the cathedral. I would watch over him and make sure he did not get himself into too much mischief or that he hurt himself running amongst the stones.

Once, as he sat alone in the courtyard one day, he appeared to be very bored and looked to be near the point of tears. I quickly went to my secret stash, and not long after little Arlo found a wooden horse to play with. The smile and laughter this child displayed as he imagined himself running through the grand, green fields of grass was something anyone would enjoy. It was as if the child was running alongside the wild stallion that he held in his small, pale hand. I enjoyed every second of that day. It was one I cherished. I truly wish I knew how Arlo had done in life after the war.

Beginning in 1940 and lasting the next five years, war would be not just some tragic event happening elsewhere in the world, but on our doorstep. England was bombed in city and in countryside by the Nazi Empire. The Luftwaffe flew over the English skies in the night and dropped bombs and bullets. Fear spread throughout the country like a wildfire.

Lincoln was not spared of any of it; fear, bombs, and bullets all were present in the city.

There were times when Lincoln was bombed. Houses were destroyed, a number of people killed while they slept. Some unfortunates died while running to shelter. Tragedy sank deep into the hearts of those in Lincoln and Lincolnshire.

One night, as the bombing was happening from above, I watched from the rooftops as several families ran towards the cathedral for safety. Mothers and fathers held their childrens' hands as they guided them to the safe refuge that the church could provide them.

One of the children was holding a teddy bear, I believe, when she dropped it. The child tried to turn back to grab her beloved teddy, but her mother stopped her. The child's older sister turned back instead, assuring her younger sister that she would grab the toy for her. And that was that. The end of a life while trying to do a good deed for a loved one.

There are times when I curse this sort of gift I have with sensing death. As soon as the sister turned back, I instantly looked up and the bomb that left the underbelly of the German bomber. The Germans apparently thought it funny to write the words "Auf Wiedersehen" on the bomb. I was never more sad to see those words. It was the exact opposite of funny.

The bomb fell quickly (although in the moment the bomb seemed to fall incredibly slow), and made impact with the ground not far from the poor girl. If I had to guess, she was thirteen or fourteen years old. Her death was quick and painless, but the pain the mother felt upon seeing her daughter's end was the worst thing I've ever seen. She froze at first, almost as if she was hoping it didn't happen. If she blinked, her daughter would reappear in front of her, holding that damn teddy bear.

The poor woman's husband came to her aid and grabbed her hand, shouting that they needed to get the rest of their children to safety. They made it thank...I don't know. I don't know if I can give credit to God, but I know that the Devil enjoyed this type of misery. I've begun to hate that.

Anyway, I remember a dread coming to me as I thought about little Arlo and the wooden horse I had left with him. I hoped and found myself wishing aloud that he would not turn back for the toy if bombing was going on around him.

After the bombings began to subside due to the war turning in favor of the Allies, things were better but people were still miserable as wartime made life difficult for the people at home and they waited every day to hear that their loved ones were safe and sound on the front.

VE Day was a glorious day. It took awhile, but that wonderful May day in 1945 brought a lot of relief and happiness. It was not a

day of wine for me, but cold,
delicious beer. I had several
pints of Guinness, and a very nice
local XB bitter from Batemans.
Went great with fish and chips.
That night I did not just drink
for the victory. I drank to all
those who suffered. To those who
lived, to those who died, and to
those lived and wanted to die.
That war taught me something. I
just wish that it had taught
humans something.

Chapter 14: 2018 - EFL Trophy Final

_____I am jumping ahead a ways,
closer to the present day. Don't
worry we're close to the end of
what is happening that has
inclined me to write my memoirs to
begin with. Before I finally get
to that, I have to brag about
something. Did you know that the
city of Lincoln has a football
team? (For you Americans that's
what everyone else in the world
calls soccer). And were aware that
this football team's mascot, logo,

and team name is me? Yes, the
Lincoln City FC Imps. That's
right. The city has come to honor
me and is proud of me, the little
statue on their cathedral.

Now my team is not in the
Premier League (yet) but they do
alright! In fact in 2018, the team
not only won League Two, but they
also won the EFL Trophy. What a
year! I obviously can't watch the
games in person, but I've managed
to watch highlights and even the
occasional live stream using the
wifi. Yes I know what wifi is. In
fact, I had to teach Nathan how to
use it. He won't admit that, but
it's true. He fought the new
technology for decades, but I
finally convinced him how useful
it was.

Nathan: I need to get on Headbook.
Me: Facebook, Nate. It's called
Facebook.
Nathan: Whatever. I want to get on
it and talk face to face with
another angel.
Me: Oh my God, Nate. That's
Facetime!

Nathan: Whatever! Open it. And then go away.

   Anyway, in 2018 the people kept coming to the church, praying and praying. Although, they weren't dressed up in their typical Sunday clothes. They wore red and white all over and football scarves with an image of me worn around their necks. They prayed that their team would win the league, that they would win this trophy and that trophy. They poured their hearts and souls into these prayers and wishes. Nathan told me God has nothing to do with such trivial matters like football, but I felt he misunderstood the point of it all.
   Football is not just sport. It's much more. It's life, it's love, and it's togetherness all combined into one cultural event. A local club is not a team to watch, it's something that causes us to celebrate when they win or cry in despair when they lose.
   I often recall watching Imps fans marching through the streets

after a victory, celebrating and
drinking a pint to make the night
more and more memorable. I would
often join them in their
celebrations. I'd enjoy a pint of
English or Scottish ale, partaking
in some fish and chips from the
rooftops, singing the songs of the
club and admiring the glory of the
occasion.

My favorite occasion was the
day we won the EFL Trophy. Lincoln
City FC won 1-0 against
Shrewsbury. How I wish I could
have been there at Wembley in
London, taking in the wonders and
spectacles of the match and seeing
that marvelous end result when the
final whistle blew. But instead I
watched it online from a laptop
I'd stolen from some tourists
visiting the cathedral. I sat
nervously drumming my stone
fingers on the table, pint number
three in my other hand when the
one and only goal of the match was
scored. That ball hitting the net
for your team makes one happy
indeed. What followed then was
seventy-four plus minutes of

anxiety and rage. Waiting for that final whistle was torture, but as the final seconds were ticking away, I jumped up and down, ready for that sweet relief of victory and greatness. I drank a lot that evening, ecstatic that our team had won its incredible match, and ending what had become an amazing season.

I want to reveal that I may have had something to do with that victory. I will explain. As an imp, or minion of the Devil, I have powers that are difficult to explain to your puny minds. Just know that I have powers (a curse of gift depending on the day) and that those powers can be transferred to others if I so choose. In the past I may have temporarily let others borrow my powers, including Captain John Smith, Sir Issac Newton, and several others.

Well in 2018 I may have lent some of that power/athleticism to one or two of the players on the team as they walked by the cathedral leading up to the semifinals and finals of the tournament. Is that cheating? Of course not. The football team honors me by choosing me as their logo and naming themselves "the imps", so I must in return honor them, no?

I am proud to call the Imps my team and I know that they represent the great city of Lincoln. "I'm City 'til I die!"

Chapter 15: Rule Breaker, Present Day

"Stop. Don't go."

The girl froze and looked back. She was scared, especially when she didn't see anyone.

"Hello? Who's there?"

I wasn't sure how to proceed from here. I sort of hoped that maybe I could just talk to her and not have to reveal myself, but I could see that she needed to see someone in order for her to stay any longer.

"My name is Linc. I know why you're here and I thought you could stay here for the night."

"Are you a ghost?"

"What? A ghost? No, ghosts aren't real, girl."

"Then where are you? Why can't I see you?"

"Ugh." I sighed aloud, not having planned this. I am such a good planner and here I am having to completely improvise. Not to mention my Christmas Eve plans have gone out the window.

"Listen, not to sound creepy but it's really for the best that you don't see me."

"Why?"

"So...many...questions. Alright look, I'm not supposed to show myself, so can you just trust me on this or do you need to see me to stay?"

The girl shook her head, taking a step back, making it clear that was not acceptable to her. I sighed again and stepped out to where she could see me properly. She gasped. She didn't turn and run away like I thought she would. After her initial reaction, she looked at me quizzically, most likely wondering if I was some kind of new toy that could talk or someone wearing a costume.

"What are you?"

"Okay, look. If you stop asking questions and just sit down, I'll tell you who I am. Want some water? You should probably have some."

I walked over to the refrigerator and grabbed a water bottle, thinking of what the hell I was going to say next to this human. All my conversations in life had been with demons, Nathaniel the angel, and myself. As I stood there, stalling, she started asking questions...again.

"Are you a gargoyle?"

"What? No!" I shook my head. "Alright girl. Wait, first tell me your name. I'm tired of saying girl or human."

"My name is Lily."

"Fine. Lily. Well, Lily, I am not a gargoyle. I'm an imp.

"Oh! Like - "

"No, not that kind of imp. That's a rude, derogatory term for people of short stature and is not acceptable. Anyway, I'm an imp, or a demon. A stone imp demon."

"My dad wears shirts with pictures of you on them."

"Well you just sort of ruined that for me."

"How are you alive?"

"Read the book someday kid. It's way too long of a story to tell you now. For now, let's just say that I was turned to stone by a high and mighty angel and I've lived here for a very long time."

"So are you my guardian angel?"

"No. Far from it. I am an imp who wreaks havoc on the world and all its inhabitants."

Lily just looked at me, confused as she ate the last of the blueberry muffins.

"Listen, I know what is going on in your life. You come here to cry it out and then you go back home. Tonight, I figured, since it's Christmas Eve, you shouldn't have to go back to that and have a nice Christmas."

Lily nodded. As if saying the words would make him appear out of thin air. I decided it would be best to move on and let her forget about her troubles for now.

"Alright Lily. What's your favorite Christmas movie?"

She beamed. She looked at me right in the eyes and yelled, "the Grinch!"

"I knew I liked you kid. Excellent choice."

As I set up the movie on my laptop (yes I have a laptop but I like to type on the typewriter when possible), I couldn't help but ask.

"So, Lily. How come you didn't run? When you saw me?"

"You gave me hot chocolate and food, and made me a bed. You must be very nice!"

"But aren't you scared of my appearance?"

"No not really."

"How old are you?"

"Nine."

"Hmm. My guess was pretty close."

"Can I pet you?"

"NO."

I put the movie on, got her
some more water and some
strawberries to munch on if she
wanted (since she'd been eating
nothing but baked goods), and then
sat down at the kitchen table.
Lily would occasionally look over
in my direction, but for the most
part she watched the movie. She
sang the famous Grinch song,
laughed at Max, and smiled at the
end when the Grinch was all happy
and friends with everyone.

She had begun yawning near
the end of the story, and when it
did end, she laid her head down on
a pillow. She was clearly
exhausted and close to sleep. I
went over to put the blankets over
her so she'd be warm throughout
the night, and as I went over to
the fireplace to keep it going,
she said, "thank you Linc. You're
a good person."

Me. A good person. Who knew?
When I looked back at her, she was
out for the count. I felt a sense
of pride for doing something for
this little girl, but I knew at
some point something would have to

be done eventually. How was this abused child supposed to return home to a father who beated her on a daily basis?

I made the decision that I would give her a very special Christmas morning at least. I found an old stocking and filled it with candies, cards, some money, and a fidget spinner (I HATE those things) some kid had left at the cathedral one day. Then I went to secret stash and found an unopened Nintendo Switch with Mario Kart (what I have an Amazon account). I wrapped it up and placed it next to the stocking not far from the fireplace. In the morning I'd bake some cinnamon rolls for her and some peppermint tea. Unless she drinks coffee. When is it appropriate to let a child drink coffee?

After all this, I grabbed my typewriter and have written these last two chapters. I looked through the many pages I've typed up about my life here at the cathedral. There's a whole lot more I could've written down, but

I wasn't sure it'd all be interesting to anyone who read this someday, if it ever is read.

I am not sure what tomorrow will bring. For all I know, Nate will find out and I'll be set in stone permanently, for all eternity, never to move or speak again. I hope that doesn't happen. But if it does, I can at least go knowing that I did something for someone other than myself. Children are the future people, and they deserve to be cherished, well nurtured, and loved. If you can't do that, then screw you. So I possibly end this story with one last statement.

Sometimes...humans suck.

Chapter 16: The End

Hello Reader,

This is Nathaniel. Yes, Nathaniel the angel that the imp has referred to often in the story. I regret to inform you that Linc is no more. He has been set in stone for all eternity for breaking the sacred rule. Now

please know, this was not my
doing. Yes, I did originally turn
him to stone, but once that was
done, I was no longer involved.
Linc's predicament was between him
and God. So please don't blame me.

   I felt that Linc deserved to
have the end of his story told in
some manner, so here it is.

   On the morning of Christmas,
I came upon him cooking in the
kitchen, with the child sleeping
in a bed he had clearly made for
her. I decided not to make my
presence known at the time,
deciding to see what was
happening. The child woke up to
the smell of cinnamon and coffee,
something the imp liked to have
every Christmas morning since some
time in the 1900's. When she
discovered the stocking and
present, she squealed with
delight. She had never gotten a
Christmas present before. After
opening the present, she ran over
and hugged the imp, thanking him
over and over again. He was
clearly embarrassed by this show
of emotion. He pretended that he

hated it and told the girl to go eat her breakfast, but in reality he very much enjoyed it. He had never been shown any kindness such as that.

After Lily (as I heard him call her) ate her breakfast and had some peppermint coffee, Linc helped set up her game device that he had given her for the holiday. I told him to stop using the cathedral's online accounts to acquire things he liked, but I guess that's all moot now. As the child played her game, a great noise came from elsewhere in the cathedral. Doors were banging, shouting could be heard. The girl, terrified, shuddered and hid under the kitchen table. Linc the imp immediately comforted her, telling her all would be right. I saw him grab a cell phone (I wasn't aware he had one) and make a call (who does he know that has a phone?). It was a brief call, and after he hung up, he assured the girl again (he revealed her name was Lily), and went off.

Lily kept very quiet under the table, until her fear took over. She got out from under the table and went out a separate door. I followed her, my curiosity getting the better of me and wondering what all of this was about. She came into the church, and it was there that I came to see what was causing all of the ruckus. A man in his forties stood there in the middle of the pews, spewing awful words I shall not repeat and demanding where Lily was. She hid herself behind the altar at hearing her name.

The man was not fat but was certainly on his way there, most likely due to drinking alcohol too much. His hair was thinning and beginning to show greys throughout the brown hair of his. He clearly had a mean temper and was drunk. This was a man who was suffering, but I could tell that he took a turn for the worst, and I feared that this poor girl was the one suffering because of it.

As Lily began to crawl to another part of the church,

possibly hoping to find a way around the man, obviously her father, he noticed her. He screamed her name and demanded that she come over to him right away. When she hesitated, he threw a bottle in her direction.

"How dare you not come when I call you! Where were you last night? Why didn't you come home?"

Before Lily had a chance to reply, he shouted, "answer me!"

Lily began to cry. She hugged herself and rocked back and forth, as if she hoped she would begin to roll away from this place forever. At this, the father lost his control. He stormed up towards the altar, saying more curse words. Before reaching her, he grabbed one of the candlesticks from atop to the altar, and swung it back, ready to strike the girl on her head.

Before I knew it, Linc the Imp came from above, screaming. It was frightening for anyone, including me. It was like a shrill, like a lout soul or banshee was coming out of the wilderness, terrifying any poor human soul who heard it for the rest of their short lives.

Linc came down onto the father's head, and they both went down onto the ground. The father had some blood coming from his head, but he was not dead. He was near unconsciousness, but not quite. Linc had rolled away after impact and went over to Lily. He told her all would be alright. I was most surprised by what happened next. Linc softly put his head against hers, and then mumbled something that I could not hear. The girl smiled and hugged him.

As the father lay groaning, he slowly turned his head towards the pair. His eyes widened when he saw a stone imp sitting there next to his daughter. Linc, noticing this, crawled towards the father on all fours in a way that was slightly unnerving. The father shivered, as if a spider was crawling on him. When Linc got to the father's face, he put his mouth right up to him, and showing his teeth, said most venomously, "You will NEVER touch her again. If you do, I will do the most foul things to you that even your nightmares cannot imagine them. You will be better or I shall come after you in the night."

The father whimpered, and tears rolled down his cheeks. He turned his head the other way, hoping the nightmare would end.

Linc stood, looked at Lily, and gave her a wave. She smiled again at him and thanked him. He then walked over to the stone pillar I had first cast him into stone on. I followed him, wondering what on earth he was up to.

He then sat up on the pillar, crossed his right leg over his left and laid his hands on them. It was then that I saw the transformation happening. He was turning into an unmovable stone permanently. He started from his feet and was heading upwards to his horns. I realized that by interacting with the humans, he had broken the rule. He was facing the consequences. I was sad to see it occurring. I was sorry to see Linc, this most annoying imp, going away. I would miss him sometimes. As his transformation was almost complete, he noticed me for the first time, and winked. And then he was gone. And that was that. May Linc the Imp rest in peace.

Chapter 16: Afterward (Written by the author)

On Christmas Day, after Nathaniel saw Linc turn to stone permanently, the police came and found the father and Lily in the cathedral. There, next to the girl, lay a tape recorder that told the police all they needed to hear. They could hear the father threatening his child, Lily screaming, and nothing else. They arrested the father and took him away. Lily stayed at the cathedral until her grandmother (Lily's maternal grandmother) came to pick her up. Lily was happy to see her and gave her a big hug. She would be treated kindly and taken care of by her. As Lily got in the back seat of her grandmother's Cooper, she saw Linc and smiled. She blew him a kiss, and then the car drove off.

The day after Christmas, Nathaniel the angel put together all of the pages the Imp and himself had typed. He then went to the office, scanned them all, and emailed them to some self-published author in America that no one had heard of...ever. After doing so, the angel went to the roof of the cathedral and looked out over the snow covered city, taking in the view just as he used to see Linc the Imp do. He wished he had sat down and talked with the noisy little stone creature more often.

He had brewed some coffee, wanting to see what all of the fuss was about, and was about to take his first sip.

"Nate old buddy!"

Coffee went everywhere, and the angel couldn't believe what he saw. There, just behind him, was Linc the Imp.

He was speechless.

Linc chuckled. "Guess the Big Guy upstairs took kindly to what I did for Lily, huh?"

The moral of the story: Good deeds may redeem even the most mischievous creatures in this world.

About the Author:

Charles is a history teacher who lives in South Florida with his amazing wife, Laura, and their wonderful son, Finn. Chuck enjoys reading, writing, playing golf, playing video games, and watching soccer.

Made in the USA
Middletown, DE
24 June 2023

33479322R00066